T0030679

BARRACOON

ADAPTED FOR YOUNG READERS

*"In Africa soil, my mama,
she name me Kossula."*

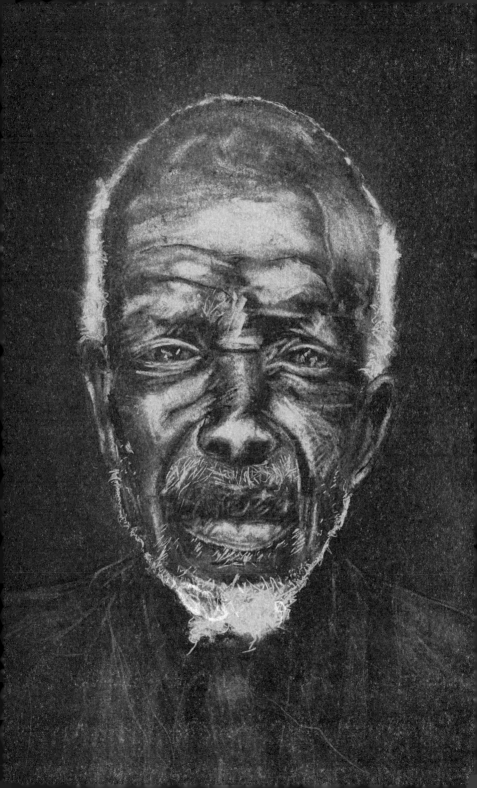

Written by
ZORA NEALE HURSTON
Author of *Their Eyes Were Watching God*

Adapted by
IBRAM X. KENDI
National Book Award Winner

Illustrated by
JAZZMEN LEE-JOHNSON

BARRACOON

ADAPTED FOR YOUNG READERS

AMISTAD
Books for Young Readers
An Imprint of HarperCollins Publishers

Amistad is an imprint of HarperCollins Publishers.

Text adapted from *Barracoon* © 2018 by Zora Neale Hurston
Text adaptation © 2024 by
The Zora Neale Hurston Trust and Ibram X. Kendi
Cover and interior illustrations © 2024 by Jazzmen Lee-Johnson

Library of Congress Control Number: 2023932837
ISBN 978-0-06-309833-6

Typography by David DeWitt
23 24 25 26 27 LBC 5 4 3 2 1

First Edition
Originally published in 2018 by Amistad

For Africa Town

CONTENTS

This is a survivor's story.

INTRODUCTION

THE TRANSATLANTIC HUMAN trade is the most dramatic chapter in the story of human existence. A great literature has grown up about it. Those who defended it have had their say. Among them are European traders who have boasted of buying and selling human flesh. All these words from the buyer and seller. Not one word from the sold.

European traders forced people in Africa onto

ships that carried them to the Americas. This scary journey is now called the Middle Passage. When enslaved people were forced onto the ships, no one told them where they were going, or whether they would ever see their families and friends and homelands again. Between 1501 and 1875, about 12.5 million people endured the Middle Passage. Nearly two million people died during the voyage. Among the more than 10 million survivors, about 300,000 of these enslaved people were sent to the United States. Of all the people transported against their wills from Africa to the United States, Cudjo Lewis was the only known person still alive in 1931.

This is the life story of Cudjo Lewis, as told by himself. It makes no attempt to be a scientific document, but on the whole, he is rather accurate. If he is a little hazy as to detail, he is certainly to be

forgiven. Cudjo Lewis tells his story in his own way, without the intrusion of interpretation.

Cudjo told his story, in his own way, to the great African American storyteller Zora Neale Hurston. She was from Eatonville, Florida, and is well known as "a genius of the South." In the 1920s and 1930s, Hurston published several novels and short stories about African Americans. Many young people are reading her novel, *Their Eyes Were Watching God*, in high schools across the United States. Hurston not only told her own stories; she collected and preserved the stories of African Americans. Perhaps the most important story she collected and preserved was the story of Cudjo Lewis.

Hurston had met Cudjo for the first time in July 1927. He lived in Plateau, Alabama, a suburb of

Mobile. She talked with Cudjo again in December of 1927 and again in 1928. Thus, from Cudjo and from research, she learned the story of the last load of enslaved people brought into the United States—the last "Black cargo."

Hurston tried to publish Cudjo's story before he died in 1935. Publishers said no. Hurston wasn't able to find a publisher before she died in 1960. *Barracoon: The Story of the Last "Black Cargo"* was not published until 2018.

Ibram X. Kendi adapted Hurston's *Barracoon* into this book. As a college professor, he writes books on African American history, racism, and being antiracist for adults and young people. Kendi has long admired the writings of Hurston, especially *Barracoon*. In this adaption, he translated Cudjo's story and Hurston's words for young people, ensuring that the narration and dialogue are read-able, understandable, and appropriate for young readers. Kendi balanced the process of making the story accessible and clear for young people with an intense focus on preserving Cudjo's voice, Hurston's voice, as well as the history, cultures, struggles, and triumphs they shared. Some of Cudjo's words are spelled differently in this adaptation, so young readers can both recognize their meaning and how Cudjo pronounced them. As Hurston sought to preserve Cudjo's voice, Kendi sought to preserve Cudjo's and Hurston's voices. Stories are passed down from generation to generation like money. But the most valuable things humans receive from the past generations are not money. They are sto-ries. The past is always present because of stories. The past is always teaching us through stories.

Cudjo was born in Africa and enslaved in the United States. Enslavers made a lot of money forcing enslaved people like Cudjo to work in fields, boats, homes, and factories without pay. Enslaved people were whipped and hurt if they didn't work, or work fast enough. They typically had little to no say in how they spent most of their days, or what they ate, drank, or wore.

Cudjo and other enslaved people did not accept their enslavement or the strict rules and punishments that came with it. They pushed back in many ways: they ran away or fought enslavers together. They sang together. They cooked together. They worshiped together. They loved together. Enslaved people were human beings, not property. The people enslaving Cudjo were being racist. They lied and said they shackled Cudjo because of the color of his skin. They lied and said Black people should be enslaved, and White people should be free. These were lies because wealthy White people enslaved Black people to make money from their labor. And lots of it.

Slavery ended in the United States in 1865, but racism did not. It remained legal to enslave people who were in prison. And soon, several states were forcing incarcerated Black people to work in fields, mines, and other places. This all happened under what became known as Jim Crow. Under Jim Crow, there were "Whites only" restaurants, bathrooms, water fountains, and many other segregated places. Black people were forced to ride at the back of buses and sit in the balcony at theatres. Few Black people could vote. Black people like Cudjo rarely received justice in the courts, and they labored for little more pay than the nothing they had received during slavery. In almost every case, Black workers received less pay than White workers for doing the same job. And there were violent organizations like the Ku Klux Klan that bullied and killed Black people to keep them down. The Klan bullied and killed people of all races who fought for equality. But the Klan could not stop the antiracist fight against Jim Crow.

The four men responsible for bringing Cudjo against his will to the United States were three brothers and Captain William "Bill" Foster. Jim, Tim, and Burns Meaher were from the state of Maine. The Meaher brothers moved from Maine to Alabama. They had a place on the Alabama River where they built fast boats. The Meahers hired Captain Foster to steer the ship. Captain Foster had done business with the Meahers. He was from Canada.

The *Clotilda* was the fastest boat available. She was the one selected to make the trip. Captain Foster seems to have been the owner of the vessel. He sailed in command and hired a crew of northern sailors.

These northern sailors led by a Canadian-born captain showed the international life of the institution of slavery in 1859. European and northern banks lent money to southern enslavers to buy enslaved people who had been taken from Africa, and to buy land that had been taken from Native people. Cotton, rice, tobacco, and sugar grown by enslaved people on southern land were often made into goods in northern and European factories. Many northerners and Europeans resisted their neighbors who called for the abolition of US slavery.

It had been illegal to import enslaved people from Africa into the United States since 1808. So, the captain lied to authorities, saying that the *Clotilda* was sailing to the coast of West Africa for red palm oil. The ship slipped away from Mobile as secretly as possible, to avoid getting in trouble.

The *Clotilda* had an uneventful voyage east in the Gulf of Mexico, through the Caribbean, and out into the Atlantic Ocean. Then a hurricane struck, and Captain Foster had to stop for repair at the Cape Verde islands off the coast of West Africa. While the ship was in dry dock, his crew got upset. They demanded more pay or they would tell authorities about the captain's illegal intentions. Captain Foster hurriedly promised more pay for the sailors, though he would later break this promise.

After the repairs had been made, Captain Foster

sailed away. Soon the ship was safely anchored in the Gulf of Guinea, off the coast of Whydah, the port of the mighty nation of Dahomey. Today, Whydah is Ouidah, a city on the coast of the Republic of Benin in West Africa. Whydah did not have a harbor where ships could dock. So, ships had to sit out at sea.

The communications with the shore were carried on by Kroo men in their surf boats. These Kroo men and boys were ship laborers who were very skilled in steering small boats filled with people or merchandise through the waves and onto the beach.

The Kroo men brought Captain Foster to the prince of Dahomey. The prince received him seated on his throne; he was gracious and hospitable.

Captain Foster had little trouble purchasing enslaved Africans. The barracoons—the jails where traders kept enslaved people—were overflowing.

For centuries, European traders had instigated wars between nations in West Africa. They knew the prisoners of war would be sold to traders. European traders created the increased demand for enslaved people.

There were numerous ethnic groups and nations in West Africa in 1859. The similarities of their darker skins hid all the different languages spoken, different religions practiced, and different political nations. When someone from one group traded someone from another group, they were not selling their *own* people. Back then, the different peoples in West Africa had no conception of being one people, of being a single Black race. Just as European human traders from Portugal and England and France had no conception of being one people.

While some nations in West Africa stayed out of

the trade of humans, other nations sold their incarcerated people to acquire guns to protect themselves against European traders and human-trading nations in West Africa. There may have been no greater human-trading nation than Dahomey.

Europeans demanded. The king of Dahomey supplied. King Ghezo maintained a standing army of twelve thousand soldiers, and about five thousand of these soldiers were women.

The Dahoman year was divided into two parts—the wars and the festivals. When Captain Foster arrived in May 1859, the wars had just finished. He had a large collection of enslaved people to choose from. He selected 130—equal numbers of men and women—paid for them, and went back to his ship. Other boats piloted by the Kroo boys carried his "property."

When 116 of the enslaved people had been brought aboard, Captain Foster became alarmed. He saw all the Dahoman ships suddenly run up black flags. He ordered his sailors to abandon the enslaved people not yet on board. He thought the Dahomans planned to take the people he'd bought and hold them for ransom. The *Clotilda* sped away.

The next day an English cruiser chased the *Clotilda*, but the crew opened the sails, and the ship gained speed and escaped. At the time, British ships patrolled the Atlantic Ocean to catch ships that were illegally carrying human cargo.

Nothing else eventful happened until the thirteenth day, when Captain Foster ordered the human cargo brought on deck so that they might stretch their arms and legs. They had been belowdeck all that time in a very small space. The ceilings in most ships that carried enslaved people from Africa to the Americas were only two and a half to three feet high. Though the space in the *Clotilda* greatly exceeded the usual space in most ships, enslaved people were cramped. It was very dark. They could barely move around. They could barely breathe. It smelled bad. There weren't any toilets. People who were seasick were throwing up. But what hurt the people most was that they missed home. They missed their parents and spouses and brothers and sisters. They missed their friends. They felt bad. The worst a human being could feel. This may have been the lowest point in human history. Many enslaved people died at sea and were thrown overboard into the Atlantic Ocean.

When Captain Foster reached US waters, the enslaved people were put back in the small hold.

The *Clotilda* arrived in Mobile on a Sunday morning in August 1859, having taken seventy days to make the trip. The last known ship with human cargo was at the end of its voyage. The *Clotilda* secretly arrived in the cover of night at Twelve-Mile Island outside of Mobile, Alabama. Then, the Meahers smuggled the enslaved Africans up the river.

Captain Foster stayed back at Twelve-Mile Island. He tried to destroy the *Clotilda*, burning the evidence of the illegal activity. Captain Foster regretted it. The ship was priced higher than the ten Africans given to him by the Meahers for payment.

The enslaved Africans were kept at the plantation of a man named John Dabney for eleven days. They could only whisper. They were constantly moved from place to place. Finally, they arrived at the Bend in Clark County. It is a place where the Alabama and the Tombigbee Rivers come together. It is where Burns Meaher had a plantation.

Meaher secretly sent word to people interested in buying enslaved Africans. Some couples were bought and taken to Selma, Alabama. The remainder were divided up among the Meahers and Captain Foster. Jim Meaher took thirty-two (sixteen couples), Burns Meaher took ten people, Captain Foster received ten, and Captain Tim Meaher took eight.

After a period of adjustment, the enslaved people were put to work. Before a year had passed, the Civil War, a conflict primarily fought over slavery, broke out.

Before long, authorities discovered that the Meahers had broken the law. They were tried in the federal courts in 1860 and 1861 and fined a lot of money for illegally bringing enslaved people into the country. But the victims of this injustice did not receive justice. The US did not return Cudjo and the other people taken back to their homes in Africa.

After the Civil War, these Africans built a village. They called it AfricaTown. The town is now called Plateau, Alabama. The new name was bestowed upon it by a company that built railroad tracks through the town. But still its dominant tone is African.

With these things already known to her, Hurston once more sought the ancient house of the man called Cudjo. This singular man who says of himself, "Edem etie ukum edem etie upar": the tree of two woods, literally, two trees that have grown together. One part ukum (mahogany) and one part upar (ebony). He means to say, "Partly a free man, partly free." The only man in the United States who has in his heart the memory of his African home, the horrors of human beings being stolen, the barracoon, the toil and terror of slavery, and who has sixty-seven years of freedom in a foreign land behind him.

How does one sleep with such memories beneath the pillow? Hurston went to ask.

This is the story of Cudjo Lewis, as told to us by Zora Neale Hurston, who talked to him a century ago.

"I want to ask you
many things. I want
to know who you are
and how you came
to be enslaved. . . ."

—*ZORA NEALE HURSTON*

Chapter One

AFRICA

IT WAS SUMMER when I went to talk with Cudjo in 1927. His door was standing wide open. But I knew he was somewhere about the house before I entered the yard.

I hailed him by his African name as I walked up the steps to his porch. He looked up into my face as I stood in the door in surprise. He was eating his breakfast from a round pan with his hands, in the fashion of his homeland.

The surprise of seeing me halted his hand between pan and face. Then came his tears of joy.

"Oh Lor', I know it you call my name. Nobody don't call-ee me my name from cross de water but you. You always call-ee me Kossula, jus' like in Africa!"

Cudjo always spoke to me in that familiar African American English, or Ebonics, which is still spoken by many African Americans. He did not speak "broken" English—just like English is not "broken" German or Latin. English is the child of Germanic and Latin languages. Cudjo speaks a language that enslaved people from West Africa created in the United States out of their own languages and English. Cudjo sounds -*ee* and -*as* and -*es* at the end of many words. He drops the *g* at the end of words ending in -*ing*, as in *nothin'*. He uses *d* in place of *th*

in words, like *de* instead of *the*, or *dis* instead of *this*. He'll also say *doan* instead of *don't*.

I saw another man eating with him and I wondered why. So I said, "I see you have company, Kossula."

"Yeah, I got to have somebody stay wid me. I been sick in de bed de five months. I need-a somebody hand me some water. So I take dis man and he sleep here and take care Cudjo," he said. He sometimes refers to himself in the third person, calling out his own name.

"But I get well now."

In spite of his recent illness and trouble accessing water, I found Cudjo Lewis full of goodwill. His garden was planted. There was deep shade under his China-berry tree.

He wanted to know a few things about New

York. When I had answered him, he sat silently. I told him I had come to talk with him. He smiled.

"I like have company come see me," he said. His smile went away. "I so lonely. My wife she left me since de 1908. Cudjo all by his-self."

After a minute or two he remembered me and said, "Excuse me. You didn't do nothin' to me. Cudjo feel so lonely. He can't help he cry sometime. What you want wid me?"

"First, I want to ask you how you feel today?" Silence. Then he said, "I thank God I on prayin' ground and in a Bible country."

"But didn't you have a God back in Africa?" I asked him. His head dropped between his hands and the tears fell. Seeing the sadness in his face, I felt bad. He read my face and said, "Excuse-ee me, I cry. I can't help it when I hear de name call. Oh,

Lor'. I no see Africa soil no more!"

Another long silence. Then, "How come you askin' me if we had God back in Africa?"

"Because you said, 'Thank God you were on praying ground and in a Bible country.'"

"Yeah, in Africa we always know dere was a God; he name Alahua. But nobody tell us about Adam eat-ee de apple. Our parents don't tell us dat. Dey didn't tell us about de first days. So dat whut you come asking me?"

I hesitated. "Well, yes. I wanted to ask that, but I want to ask you many things. I want to know who you are and how you came to be enslaved; and to what part of Africa do you belong, and how was enslavement for you, and how you have managed as a free man?"

His head bowed for a time. He lifted his wet

face. He said, "Thank-ee Jesus! Somebody come ask about Cudjo! I want tell-ee somebody who I is, so maybe dey go in de Africa soil some day and call-ee my name and somebody dere say, 'Yeah, I know Kossula.' I want you everywhere you go to tell everybody whut Cudjo say, and how come I in American soil since de 1859 and never see my people no more.

"My name is not Cudjo Lewis. It Kossula. In Africa soil, my mama, she name me Kossula.

"My people in Africa, you understand me, dey not rich. Thass de truth, now. I not goin' tell-ee you my folks dey rich and come from high blood. Den when you go in de Africa soil an' ask de people, dey say, 'Why Kossula over dere in America soil tell-ee de folks he rich?' I tell-ee you like it is. Now, thass right, ain' it?

"My father's father, you understand me, he a officer of de king. He don't live in de compound wid us. Wherever de king go, he go, you understand me. De king give him plenty land, and got plenty cows and goats and sheep. Now, thass right. Maybe after while he be a little chief, I don't know. But he die when I a lil boy.

"My grandpa, he a great man. I tell-ee you how he go." I was afraid that Cudjo might go off on a tangent, so I cut in with, "But Kossula, I want to hear about you and how you lived in Africa."

He gave me a look full of pity and asked, "Where is de house where de mouse is de leader? In de Africa soil I can't tell-ee you 'bout de son before I tell-ee you about de father; and derefore, you understand me, I can't talk 'bout de man who is father till I tell-ee you 'bout de man who he father to him.

"My grandpa, you understand me, he got de great big compound. His house, it is in de center de compound.

"When he sleeps, somebody stand guard before de door so nobody make noise and wake him. Sometime de son of an enslaved person in de compound make too much noise. De man that stand guard catch him and take him to my grandpa. He sit up and look-ee at de boy so. Den he ask him, 'Where is dat Portuguese man?' My grandpa say dat, but he don't never ask de chief to sell-ee nobody to de Portuguese.

Maybe he was thinking about the Portuguese human traders as he looked out over his patch of pole beans towards the house of his daughter-in-law. I waited for him to resume, but he just sat there not seeing me. I waited but not a sound. He turned to the man sitting inside the house and said, "Go fetch-ee me some cool water."

The man took the pail and went down the path between the rows of pole beans to the well in the daughter-in-law's yard. He returned, and Kossula gulped down a healthy cupful from a homemade tin cup.

Then he sat and smoked his pipe in silence. He seemed to discover that I was still there. He said brusquely, "Go leave me 'lone. Cudjo tired. Come back tomorrow. Doan come in de mornin' 'cause den I be in de garden. Come when it hot, den Cudjo sit in de house."

So I left Cudjo sitting in his door. His bare feet were exposed to the cloud of mosquitoes that swarmed in the shade of the inside of his house.

"I don't forget nothin'."

—CUDJO LEWIS

Chapter Two

KING

THE NEXT DAY about noon, I was again at Kossula's gate. I brought a gift this time. A basket of Georgia peaches. He received me kindly and began to eat the peaches at once. Mary and Martha, the twin daughters of his granddaughter, came up to the steps. The old man's love of these children was obvious. With glad eyes, he selected four of the finest peaches and handed two to each little girl. He asked them to go off and play. When they were gone, he looked lovingly after them and pointed to a little clump of sugarcane in the garden.

"See dat cane?" he asked. I nodded that I did.

"Well, I plant dat cane. Not much, but I grow dat so when Martha and Mary come to me and say, 'Gran'pa, I want-ee some cane,' I go cut and give 'em."

There is a large peach tree in the yard that bears small but delicious clingstone peaches. They were beginning to ripen. The old man gave me one or two and put away one for each of the twins.

I was shown all over the gardens. Kossula was friendly, but not one word about himself fell from his lips. So I went away and came again the following day. I brought another gift. A box of Bee Brand insect powder to burn in the house to drive out all the mosquitoes.

He was in a vocal mood and could not wait to talk about his Africa. So we settled on the porch and he talked. I reminded him that he had been telling me about his grandfather.

"I don't forget nothin'. I remember everything since I de five year old.

"Yeah, my grandpa, he a officer of de king. He be wid de king everywhere he go, you understand me."

"One day, a man killed a leopard. Well, de king don't care about he kill a leopard. But de law say dat when a man kill a leopard, he got to bring it to de king.

"De king don't want take de beast away from de man, you understand me. But the king got to take de whiskers dat grow round de leopard's mouth. Dey poison, and de king don't want none of de people to get it. Some mens dey wicked, you understand me,

and dey take de hairs and make de poison. Derefore, de king say, when any man kill de leopard, he got to cover de head and bring de leopard to de king.

"Den de drums beat and call-ee all brave chiefs to come discuss dis leopard dat been kill. De king keep de head, de liver, de gall, and de skin. It all make different medicine.

"One man you know, he kill a leopard. He cover de head and tie de body to a young tree. Well, de king call all de chiefs and they come look-ee. Dey take off de cover from de head and de king look at de hairs. He see one hair it gone from de hole in de face where it grow. All de chiefs dey look-ee too. Dey see de hair ain' dere. So dey call de man.

"De king say, 'Well, you kill-ee dis beast?'

"De man say, 'Yeah, I kill him.'

"'How you kill dis leopard?'

"'Wid de spear, I kill him.'

"'Did you touch de head?'

"'No, I doan touch-ee de head at all. I only a common man and I know de head belong to de king. So I doan touch it.'

"De king look-ee at de head and look-ee at de man. He say, 'How is it dis beast got de hole for de hair but one hair not dere. Tell me where de hair is. I see where it pull out. Who is it dat you want to kill?'

"De man say, 'I doan want to hurt-ee nobody. I ain' touch-ee de hair. Dat's de truth now. If I touch-ee de hair, I be in trouble.'

"Well, dey search de man and find de hair. Den dey try him. Dey find him guilty. He a wicked man that wanted to kill-ee somebody wid de hair.

"De king go back to his village, but de chief have court every day. Everything be done open dere. Not so many secrets.

"One man kill-ee another one wid de spear. So dey arrested dat man an' tie his hands wid palm cord. Den dey pick up de dead man an' carry him to de public square, de marketplace, you understand.

"In Africa, you understand, if somebody steal, de chief of de village, he try him. But if a man kill-ee somebody, den dey send for de king an' he come an' decide de case. Derefore, dey send word for de king to come. When de king come, my grandfather, he come wid him."

"Befo' anybody see de king, we know he is almost dere, because we hear de drum. When a little chief travel, he go quiet, but when de king go any place, you understand me, de drum go befo' to let de people know de king come.

"De king, he takes a special seat dey bring for him an' de chiefs from de other towns, dey sit on dey stool of rank in different places aroun' de square.

"De dead man is laying on de ground in de center where everybody see him. De man dat kill him, he tied where folks kin see him too.

"Dey ask-ee de man why he kill-ee dis other one. He say de man work magic against him so his child died, an' his cows dey stay sick all de time. De king say, 'If this man work magic against you, why doan you tell de chief of de village? Why doan you tell de king? Doan you know we got law for people dat work magic? You ain' supposed to kill de man.'

"In Africa de law is de law an' no one can get excused from de law."

I did not need to ask him if anyone can get excused from the law in the United States. We both already knew.

"My father say, 'Oh de ground eats de best of everything.'"

—CUDJO LEWIS

Chapter Three

FUNERAL

"**WHEN DEY TRY** the man dat steal de leopard hair, it de time to cut grass, so it don't choke de corn. Before de grass be dry enough to burn, my grandpa he take sick in his compound. How come he take sick, Cudjo doan know. I a lil boy and I doan know why he die.

"I didn't see him after he died. Dey bury him right away so no enemy come look down in his face and harm his spirit. Dey bury him in de house. Dey dig up de clay floor and bury him. We say in de Africa soil, 'We live wid you while you alive, how come we can't live wid you after you die?' So, you know dey bury a man in his house.

"De coffin sitting dere just like he in dere. De people come fetch-u presents and place dem in de coffin. De first wife she set at de head of de coffin. When somebody came she cry. She cry with a song. De other women dey join in and cry wid her.

"De chief wife she weep-ee very loud and said, 'It is forty years since he married me, and now you find me a widow.'

"My father say, 'Oh de ground eats de best of everything.' Den he weep-ee too.

"De chief wife say, 'He was a wonderful man.' Den my father say, 'Dat is true. De ground kin prove it.'

"Den we set ourselves on de floor and de women

cover up dere faces and get quiet.

"De men sorry he dead too. Dey come bring presents and look-ee at de coffin. Dey drink palm wine and sing for him a song.

"Den somebody else come, and de chief wife, she rise and start de weepin' again. It very sad. Derefore, you understand me, everybody feel sad.

"Dey call my grandpa brave. Den dey cry with another song:

> *Whoever shake de leaf of dat tree*
> *We are still smelling it.*
> *Whoever kill our husband,*
> *We shall never forget.*"

Kossula got that remote look in his eyes, and I knew he had withdrawn within himself.

I arose to go. "You going very soon today," he commented.

"Yes," I said, "I don't want to wear out my welcome. I want you to let me come and talk with you again."

"Oh, I don't care you come see me. Cudjo like have company. Now I go water de tater vines. You see kin you find ripe peach on de tree and get some to take home."

I put the ladder in the tree and climbed up in easy reach of a cluster of pink peaches. He saw me to the gate and said goodbye.

"Doan come back till de next week. Now I need chop-ee grass in de garden."

"I like to hear stories too. Do you remember any of the stories your mama told you?"

—ZORA NEALE HURSTON

Chapter Four

BOY NO MO'

IN THE SIX DAYS between my visits to Kossula, I worried that he might not keep talking to me. I had picked up two Virginia hams on my trip south. When I appeared before him the following Thursday, I brought him one. He was happier than he could say, but I read his face and it was more than enough. The ham was for *him*. For *us* I brought a huge watermelon, right off the ice. We cut it in half and we ate as much as we were able.

Then it was necessary to walk it off. So he showed me over the Old Landmark Baptist Church, at his very gate, where he is sexton. A sexton is an officer of a church who cleans the building and graveyard.

Watermelon, like too many other gorgeous things in life, goes much too fast. We returned to the porch.

"Now, you want me to tell-ee you some mo' about what we do in de Africa soil? Well, you good to me. I tell-ee you somethin'. It too hot [to] work anyhow.

"My father he name O-lo-loo-ay. He not a rich man. He have three wives.

"My mama she name Ny-fond-lo-loo. She de second wife. Now dat's right. I no tell-ee you I de son of de [first] wife. Dat ain' right. I de son of de second wife.

"My mama have one son befo' me so I her second

60

child. She have four mo' children after me, but dat ain' all de children my father got.

"In de compound I play games wid all de children my father got. We wrestle wid one another. We see which one can run de fastest. We climb de palm tree wid coconut on it and we eat-ee dat. We go in de woods and hunt de pineapple and banana and we eat-ee dat too. Know how we find de fruits? By de smell.

"Sometimes our mama say we play enough. Dey tell us, 'Come set down and I tell-ee you stories,' Cudjo like very much to listen."

I said, "I like to hear stories too. Do you remember any of the stories your mama told you?"

"Well," said Kossula, "I tell-ee you de story next time you come set wid me. Now I tell-ee you about Cudjo when he a boy back in de Africa.

"One day de chief send word to de compound. He want [to] see all de boys dat done see fourteen rainy seasons. Dat make-ee me very happy because I think he goin' send me to de army. I then almost fifteen rainy seasons old.

"But in de Africa soil dey teach-ee de boys long time befo' dey go in de army. Derefore, you understand me, when de boy about fourteen dey start train him for de war. Dey don't go fight right away. No, first dey got to know how to walk in de bush and see and not show dey-self. Derefore, first de elders take de boys on journey to hunt. Sometime it go and come back befo' night. Sometime it two, three nights.

"Dey got to learn to follow the tracks. Dey got to know whether whut dey hunt turned this way or that way. Dey learn to break-ee de branch and turn it so dey kin find de way back home. Dey got to knot de long leaf so de folks behind kin know to follow.

"Me make de hunt many time. We shoot de arrows from de bow. We kill de beasts and bring dem home wid us.

"I so glad I goin' be a man and fight in de army lak my big brothers. I like beat-ee de drum too.

"Dey teach-ee us to sing de war song. We sing when we walk in de bush and make like we goin' fight de enemy. De drum talk-ee wid us when we sing de song, 'Ofu, ofu, tiggy, tiggy, tiggy, tiggy batim, ofu ofu, tiggy tiggy, tiggy, tiggy batim! Ofu batim en ko esse!'" That means, "When we get there we shall make our demands, and if we are crossed we shall tear down the nation who defies us."

"Every year dey teach-ee us mo' war. But de king, Akia'on, say he don't go make no war. He make us strong so nobody don't make war on us. We know de secret of de gates so when de enemy come and we don't know dey come, we kin run hide-ee ourself in de bush. Den we come behind dem and fight.

"Four, five rainy seasons it keep on like dat. Den I grow tall and big. I can run in de bush all day and not be tired."

Kossula stopped speaking and looked at his watermelon. There was still lots of good red meat and a quart or two of juice. I looked at mine. I had more meat left than Kossula had. So we lifted the watermelon to our knees and started all over again. The sun was still hot so we did the job leisurely.

A long silence fell on us. When I was able to speak, somehow the word *juju* came into my mind, so I asked Kossula what he knew about it. He seemed reluctant to answer my question, but finally he did so.

"I tell-ee you whut I know about de juju. Whut de old folks do in de juju house, I doan know. I can't tell-ee you dat. I too young. Dat doan reach-ee me. I know dat all de grown men dey go to de mountain once a year. It have something to do wid makin' de weather, but whut dey do dere, Cudjo doan know. Now, dat's right. I doan make out I know whut go on wid de grown folks. When I come away from Africa I only a boy nineteen year old. I have one initiation. A boy must go through many initiations before he become a man. I jus' initiate one time.

"One day I was in de marketplace when I see a pretty girl walk past me. She so pretty I follow her a little way, but I doan speak. We doan do dat in Africa. But I like-ee her. One old man, he saw me watch-ee de girl. He doan say nothin' to me, but he went to my father an' say, 'Your boy is about breakin' de corn. He is getting to be a man. So put goats down or a cow an' let us fix a banquet for him.' So my father say, 'Alright.'

"But first dey doan fix de banquet for me. Dey have in Africa a small stick on a string an' when dey make it go around fast, it roar like de lion or de bull. Dey have three kinds of [bull roarers]. One, dey call it de 'he,' one de 'she,' and one dey call it de dog 'cause dey make it bark dat way.

"Dey put me in de initiation house. After a while I hear a great roaring outside de door an' dey say to me, 'Go see where dat is.' Soon's I went outside I doan hear it at de door no more. It sound way off in de bush. They tell me to go in de bush to hunt it. As soon as I go to de bush to find out whut it is, I hear it behind me. I hear it behind me, in front of me, everywhere, but I never find it. De men are playing wid me. Way after while, dey take me into de banquet an' tell me de secret of de thing dat make de sound.

"At de banquet dey make me sit an' listen wid respect. Dey tell me, 'You are jus' below us. You are not yet a man. All men are still fathers to you.'

"There is plenty of roast meat and wine at de banquet, an' all de men dey pinch-ee my ear tight to teach me to keep de secrets. Den I get a peacock feather to wear. In American soil I see plenty women wear de peacock feather.

"When I get de peacock feather, I stand round de place where de chief talk wid de wise men. I hope dey see Cudjo and think he a grown man. Maybe dey call me to de council. De fathers doan never call me but I like-ee very much to be dere and listen when dey talk."

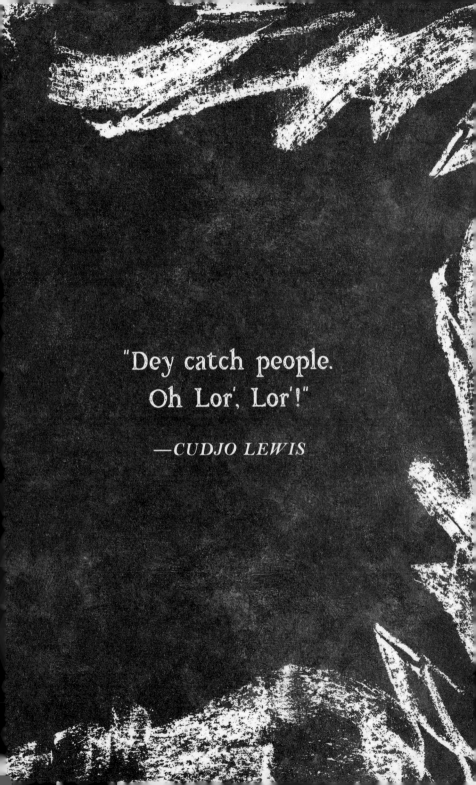

"Dey catch people.
Oh Lor', Lor'!"

—*CUDJO LEWIS*

Chapter Five

TAKEN

"**ONE DAY I** in de market, three men come [and] say dey from Dahomey and dey want-ee see our king. De king say, 'Alright, he talk wid dem.'

"Dey say, 'You know de king of Dahomey?'

"Akia'on say, 'I have heard of him.'

"De men from Dahomey say, 'Den you know all de strong names he got. You know he got one name, Tenge Makanfenkpar, a rock, the fingernail cannot scratch it, see! You know dey speak about him and say, "Kini, kini, kini, Lion of Lions." Some say, "A animal done cut its teeth, evil done enter into de bush." (The "bush," meaning the surrounding towns who feel the sharpness of Dahomey's tooth.) Dis king send to you and say he wish to be kind. Derefore you must send-ee him de half your crops. If you doan send it, he make war.'

"Our King Akia'on say, 'Ask-ee you' king did he ever hear de strong name of Akia'on? Dey call me Mouth of de Leopard? That he take hold on, he never let go. Tell him de crops ain' mine. Dey belong to de people. I can't take de people crops to send to de king of Dahomey. He got plenty land. Let him stop makin' hunt on other people and make his own crops.'

"De king of Dahomey doan like dat message, but Akia'on so strong, he afraid to come make war. So he wait.

"De king of Dahomey, you know, he got very rich catching people. He keep his army all de time making raids to grab-ee people to sell. So de people of Dahomey doan have no time to raise gardens an' make food for deyselves.

"Maybe de king of Dahomey never come make raid in Takkoi, but one traitor from Takkoi go in de Dahomey. He a very bad man and de king (of Takkoi) say, 'Leave this country.' Dat man want big honors in de army so he go straight in de Dahomey and say to de king, 'I show you how to take-ee Takkoi.' He tell-ee dem de secret of de gates.

"Derefore, you understand me, dey come make war, but we doan know dey come fight us. Dey march all night long and we in de bed sleep. We doan know nothin'.

"It bout daybreak when de folks dat sleep get

wake wid de noise when de people of Dahomey break-ee de Great Gate. I not woke yet. I still in bed. I hear de gate when dey break it. I hear de yell from de soldiers while dey chop-pee de gate. Derefore I jump out de bed and look-ee. I see de great many soldiers wid French gun in de hand and de big knife. Dey got de women soldiers too, and dey run wid de big knife and make noise. Dey catch people. Oh Lor', Lor'!

"I see de people getting kill so fast! De old ones dey try run 'way from de house but dey dead by de door. Oh, Lor'!"

Cudjo wept sorrowfully and crossed his arms on his breast with the fingers touching his shoulders. His mouth and eyes wide open as if he still saw the gruesome spectacle.

"Everybody dey run to de gates so dey kin hide

dey-self in de bush, you understand me. Some never

reach-ee de gate. De women soldier catch de young

ones and tie dem by de wrist. No man can be so

strong like de woman soldiers from de Dahomey.

I run-nee fast to de gate but some de men from

Dahomey dey dere too. I run-ee to de next gate but dey dere too. Dey surround de whole town. Dey at all de eight gates.

"One gate look-ee like nobody dere so I make haste and run-ee towards de bush. But de man of Dahomey dey dere too. Soon as I out de gate, dey grab-ee me, and tie de wrist. I beg dem, 'Please let me go back to my mama,' but dey don't pay whut I say no attention. Dey tie me wid de rest.

"While dey catching me, de king of my country he come out de gate, and dey grab-ee him. They see he de king so dey very glad. Derefore, you understand me, dey take him in de bush where de king of Dahomey wait wid some chiefs till Takkoi be destroy. When he see our king, he say to his soldiers, 'Bring me de word-changer.' When de translator came, he say, 'Ask dis man why he put his weakness against de Lion of Dahomey?' De man changed de words for our king. Akia'on listen. Den he say to de Dahomey king, 'Why don't you fight like men? Why you doan come in de daytime so dat we could meet face-to-face?' De man change-ee de words so de king of Dahomey know what he say. Den de king of Dahomey say, 'Git in line to go to Dahomey so de nations can see I conquer you and sell Akia'on in de barracoon.'

"Akia'on say, 'I ain' goin' to Dahomey. I born a king in Takkoi where my father and his fathers rule before I was born. Since I been a full man I rule. I die a king but I not be no slave.'

"De king of Dahomey ask-ee him, 'You not goin' to Dahomey?'

"He tell him no, he ain' goin' off de ground where he is de king.

"De king of Dahomey doan say no mo'. He look at de soldier and point at de king. One soldier step up and kill the king.

"When I see de king dead, I try to escape from de soldiers. I try to make it to de bush, but all soldiers overtake me befo' I git dere. O Lor', Lor'! When I think 'bout dat time I try not to cry no mo'. My eyes dey stop cryin', but de tears run-ee down inside me all de time.

"When de men pull me wid dem I call my mama name. I doan know where she is. I no see none my family. I doan know where dey is. I beg de men to let me go find-ee my folks. De soldiers say dey got no ears for cryin'. De king of Dahomey come to hunt people to sell. So dey tie me in de line wid de rest.

"De sun it jus' rising. All day dey make us walk. De sun so hot! De king of Dahomey, he ride in de

hammock. De chiefs wid him, dey got hammock too. Poor me I walk. De men of Dahomey, dey tie us in de line so nobody run off.

"I so sad for my home I ain' get hungry dat day, but I glad when we drink de water. Befo' de sun go down we come by a town. It got a red flag on de bush. De king of Dahomey send men wid de word-changer to de town and de chief come in de hammock and talk wid de king. Den he take down de red flag and hang a white flag. Whut dey say, Cudjo doan know. But he bring de king a present of yams and corn. De soldiers make fire and cook de grub and eat-ee. Den we march on. Every town de king send message.

"We sleep-ee on de ground dat night but de king and de chiefs hang dey hammock in de tree and sleep-ee in dem. Poor me I sleep-ee on de ground and cry. I ain' used to no ground. I think-ee too about my folks and I cry. All night I cry.

"When de sun rise we eat and march on to Dahomey. De king send word to every town we past and de headman come out. If dey got a red flag, dat mean dey agree dey ain' goin' pay no tax to de Dahomey. Dey say dey will fight. If it a white flag, dey pay to Dahomey whut dey ask dem. If it a black flag, dat mean dat de ruler is dead and de son not old enough to take de throne. In de African soil when dey see de black flag, dey doan bother. Dey know it be takin' advantage if dey make war when nobody in charge."

Kossula was no longer on the porch with me. He was squatting about that fire in Dahomey. His face was twitching in pain. It was a horror mask. He had forgotten I was there. He was thinking aloud and gazing into the faces in the smoke. His agony was so bad that he couldn't speak. He never noticed my preparation to leave him. I slipped away as quietly as possible and left him with his smoke pictures.

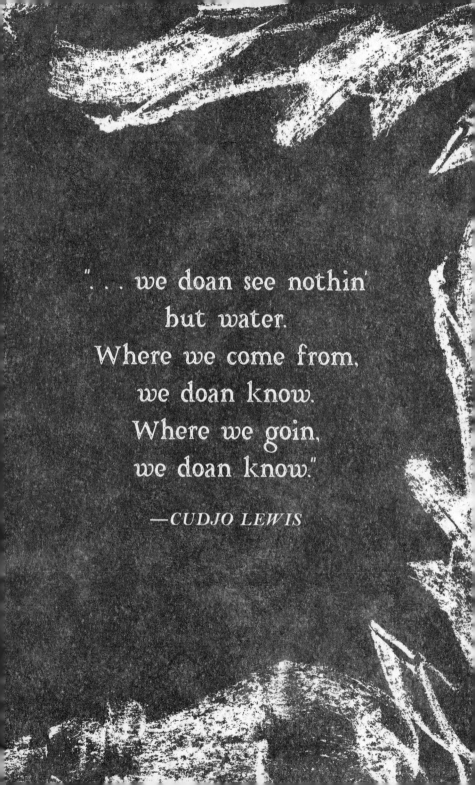

"... we doan see nothin'
but water.
Where we come from,
we doan know.
Where we goin,
we doan know."

—CUDJO LEWIS

Chapter Six

BARRACOON

IT WAS SATURDAY when I next saw Cudjo. He was gracious but not too friendly. He picked me peaches and tried to get rid of me quickly, but I hung on. Finally, he said, "Didn't I tell-ee you not to come bother me on Sat'day? I got to clean de church. Tomorrow Sunday."

"But I came to help you, Kossula. You needn't talk if you don't want to."

"I thank-ee you come help me. I want you take

me in de car in de Mobile. I get me some turnip seed to plant in de garden."

We hurriedly swept and dusted the church. Less than an hour later the Chevrolet had borne us to Mobile and back. I left him at his gate with a brief goodbye and came back again on Monday.

He was very warm this day. He shined with light.

"Dey march us in de Dahomey, and I see de house of de king. I can't tell all de towns we pass-ee to git to de place where de king got his house, but I 'member we pass-ee de place call (Meko) and Ahjahshay. We go in de city where de king got his house and dey call it Lomey. (Either Abomey or Cannah.) De house de king live in his-self, you understand me, it made out of skull bones. Maybe it not made out de skull, but it look-ee dat way to Cudjo, oh Lor'. Dey got de white skull bone on de stick when dey come meet us.

"De drum beat so much look-ee lak de whole world is de drum dey beat on. Dat de way dey fetch-ee us into de place where de king got his house.

"Dey place-ee us in de barracoon [where traders kept enslaved people] and we rest-ee ourself. Dey give us something to eat, but not very much. We stay dere three days, den dey have a feast. Everybody sing and dance and beat-ee de drum.

"We stay dere not many days, den dey march us to [the sea]. We pass a place call [Badigri]. Den we come in de place call Dwhydah [or Whydah].

"When we git in de place dey put us in a barracoon behind a big white house, and dey feed us some rice.

"We stay dere in de barracoon three weeks. We see many ships in de sea, but we can't see so good 'cause de white house. It between us and de sea.

"But Cudjo see de White men, and thass some-thin' he ain' never seen befo'. In de Takkoi we hear de talk about de White man, but he doan come dere.

"De barracoon we in ain' de only [enslaving] pen at the place. Dey got plenty of dem but we doan know who de people in de other pens. Sometime we holler back and forth and find out where each other come from. But each nation in a barracoon by itself.

"When we dere three weeks, a White man come in de barracoon wid two men of de Dahomey. One man, he a chief of Dahomey and de other one his word-changer. Dey make everybody stand in a ring—about ten folks in each ring. De men by dey-self, de women by dey-self. Den de White man look-ee and look-ee. He look-ee hard at de skin and de feet and de legs and in de mouth. Den he choose.

Every time he choose a man he choose a woman. Every time he take a woman he take a man, too. Derefore, you understand me, he take one hundred and thirty [including me]. Sixty-five men wid a woman for each man. Thass right.

"Den de White man go away. I think he go back in de white house. But de people of Dahomey come bring us lot of grub for us to eat-ee 'cause dey say we goin' leave dere.

We eat-ee de big feast. Den we cry, we sad 'cause we doan want to leave the rest of our people in de barracoon. We all lonesome for our home. We doan know whut goin' become of us. We doan want to be put apart from one another.

"But dey come and tie us in de line and lead us round de big white house. Den we see so many ships in de sea. Cudjo see many White men, too.

Dey talking wid de officers of de Dahomey. We see de White man dat buy us. When he see us ready, he say goodbye to de chief and get-ee in his hammock and dey carry him cross de river. We walk behind and wade de water. It come up to de neck and Cudjo think once he goin' drown. But nobody drown, and we come on de land by de sea. De shore it full of boats.

"De boats take something to de ships and fetch something 'way from de ships. Dey comin' and goin' all de time. Some boat got White man in it; some boat got African in it. De man dat buy us, he git in a Kroo boat and go out to de ship.

"Dey take-ee de chain off us and place-ee us in de boats. Cudjo doan know how many boats take us out on de water to de ship. I in de last boat go out. Dey almost leave-ee me on de shore. But when I see

my friend Keebie in de boat I want go wid him. So I holler and dey turn 'round and take-ee me.

"When we ready to leave de Kroo boat and go in de ship, de [Kroo boys hired by White traders] snatch our country cloth off us. We try save our clothes, we ain' used to be without no clothes on. But dey snatch all off us. Dey say, 'You get plenty clothes where you goin'. Oh Lor', I so shame! We come in de America soil naked and de people say we naked savage. Dey say we doan wear no clothes. Dey doan know dey snatch our clothes away from us.

"Soon we git in de ship dey make us lay down in de dark. We stay dere thirteen days. Dey doan give us much to eat. Me so thirst! Dey give us a little bit of water twice a day. Oh Lor', Lor', we so thirst! De water taste sour." [Human traders often added vinegar to the water to prevent a disease called scurvy. The more enslaved Africans they kept healthy on this trip, the more humans they could sell, and the more money they could make.]

"On de thirteenth day dey fetch-ee us on de deck. We so weak we ain' able to walk ourselves, so de crew take each one and walk 'round de deck till we git so we can walk ourselves.

"We look-ee and look-ee and look-ee and look-ee and we doan see nothin' but water. Where we come from, we doan know. Where we goin, we doan know.

"De boat we on called de *Clotilda*. Cudjo suffer so in dat ship. Oh Lor'! I so scared on de sea! De water, you understand me, it make so much noise! It growl like de thousand beasts in de bush. De wind got so much voice on de water. Oh Lor'! Sometime de ship way up in de sky. Sometimes it way down in

de bottom of de sea. Dey say de sea was calm. Cudjo doan know, seem like it move all de time.

"One day de color of de water change and we see some islands, but we doan come to de shore for seventy days. [Another] day we see de color of de water change and dat night we stop by de land. But we don't git off de ship. Dey send us back down in de ship and de next mornin' dey bring us de green branch off de tree so we Africans know we 'bout finish de journey.

"We been on de water seventy days and we spend some time layin' down in de ship till we tired, but many days we on de deck. Nobody ain' sick.

"Dey tell me it a Sunday and tell us to keep quiet. Captain Bill Foster, you understand me, he scared de gov'ment folks in de Fort Monroe goin' catch de ship.

"When it night, de ship move again. Cudjo didn't know den whut dey do, but dey tell me dey towed de ship up de Spanish Creek to Twelve-Mile Island. Dey took-ee us off de ship and we git on another ship. Den dey burn de *Clotilda* 'cause dey scared de gov'ment goin' arrest dem for fetchin' us away from Africa soil.

"First, dey provide us wid some clothes. Den dey carry us up de Alabama River and hide us in de swamp. But de mosquitoes dey so bad dey about to eat us up, so dey took us to Captain Burns Meaher's place and divide us up.

"Captain Tim Meaher, he took-ee thirty-two of us. Captain Burns Meaher he took-ee ten couples. Some dey sell up de river in de Bogue Chitto [in Mississippi]. Captain Bill Foster he took-ee de eight couples, and Captain Jim Meaher he get-ee de rest.

"We very sorry to be parted from one another. We cry for home. We took away from our people. We seventy days cross de water from de Africa soil, and now dey part us from one another. Derefore we cry. We can't help but cry. So we sing: 'Eh, yea ai yeah, La nah say wu Ray ray ai yea, nah nah saho ru.'

"Our grief so heavy look like we can't stand it. I think maybe I die in my sleep when I dream about my mama. Oh Lor'!"

Kossula sat silent for a moment. I saw the old sorrow seep away from his eyes and the present take its place. He looked about him for a moment and then said bluntly, "I tired talking now. You go home and come back. If I talk-ee wid you all de time I can't make no garden. You want know too much. You ask so many questions. Go on home."

I was far from being offended. I merely said,
"Well, when can I come again?"

"I send my grandson and let-ee you know, maybe
tomorrow, maybe next week."

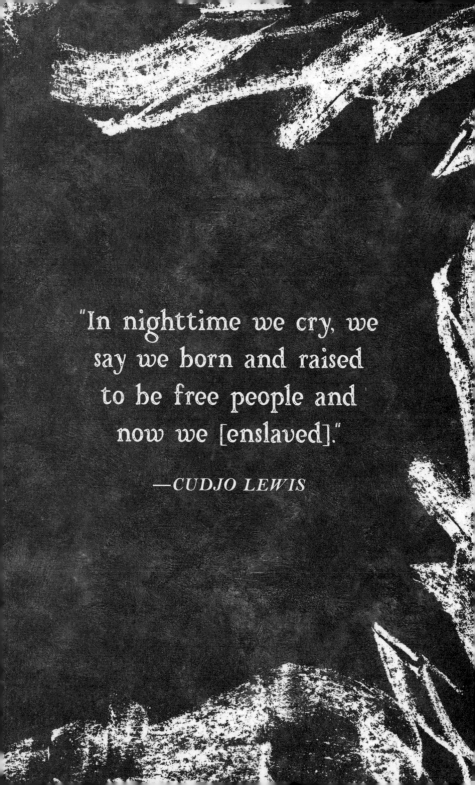

"In nighttime we cry, we say we born and raised to be free people and now we [enslaved]."

—CUDJO LEWIS

Chapter Seven

ENSLAVEMENT

"**CAPTAIN JIM, HE** took-ee me. He make a place for us to sleep-ee underneath de house. Not on de ground, you understand me. De house it high off de grounds and got de bricks underneath for de floor.

"Dey give us bed and bed cover, but ain' enough to keep-ee us warm.

"Dey doan put us to work right away 'cause we doan understand what dey say and how dey do. But de others show us how dey raise de crop in de field. We astonish to see de mule behind de plow to pull.

"Captain Tim and Captain Burns Meaher work-ee dey folks hard. Dey got overseer wid de whip. One man try whip-ee one my countrywomen and dey all jump on him and take de whip 'way from him and lash-ee him wid it. He doan never try whip African women no mo'.

"De work very hard for us to do 'cause we ain' used to work-ee lak dat. But we doan grieve about dat. We cry 'cause we [enslaved]. In nighttime we cry, we say we born and raised to be free people and now we [enslaved]. We doan know why we be bring away from our country to work like dis. It strange to us. Everybody look-ee at us strange. We want to talk wid de other colored folks but dey doan know whut we say. Some make de fun at us.

"Captain Jim, he not like his brother, Captain Tim. He doan want his folks knock and beat all de time. Now thass right. I no tell-ee lies. He work us hard, you understand me, but he doan work-ee his folks like his brother.

"Dey got de two plantation. One on de Tensaw River and one on de Alabama River.

"Oh Lor'! I appreciate dey free me! We doan have enough bedclothes. We work-ee so hard! De womens, dey work-ee in de field too. We not in de field much.

"Captain Jim got-ee five boats run from de Mobile to de Montgomery. Oh Lor'! I work-ee so hard! Every landing, you understand me, I tote wood on de boat. Dey have de [shipment], you understand me, and we have to tote dat, too. Oh Lor'! I so tired. No sleep-ee. De boat leak and we pump-ee so hard! Dey ain' got no railing on de boat. And in de nighttime if you doan watch-ee close, you fall overboard and drown yo'self. Oh Lor'! I appreciate dey free me.

"Every time de boat stop-ee at de landing, you understand me, de overseer, de whippin' boss, he go down and stand-ee on de ground. De whip stick-ee in his belt. He holler, 'Hurry up, dere, you! Run-ee fast! Can't you run-ee no faster dan dat? You ain't got enough load! Hurry up!'

"He cut-ee you wid de whip if you ain' run fast enough to please him. If you doan git a big load, he hit-ee you too. Oh, Lor'! Oh, Lor'! Five year and de six months I [enslaved]. I work-ee so hard!

"Look lak now I see all de landings after Mobile. I think I 'member dem, you understand me, but I ain' been dere since 1865. Maybe I furgit-ee some. Doan look lak I never furgit.

"I work so hard and we ain' had nothin' to sleep-ee on but de floor. Sometime de bluff it so high we got to [break] de wood down two three times before it git down where de river is. De steamboat didn't used to burn-ee de coal. It burn-ee de wood an' it

111

use so much-ee wood!

"De war commences but we doan know about it when it start. We see de White folks run-ee up and down. Dey go in de Mobile. Dey come out on de plantation. Den somebody tell me de folks way up in de North make de war so dey free us. I like hear dat. Cudjo doan want to be [enslaved]. But we wait and wait, we heard de guns shoot-ee sometime but nobody don't come tell us we free. So we think maybe dey fight about something else.

"De [Union soldiers] dey at Fort Morgan, you understand me. Dey dere on account de war and dey doan let nothin' come pass-ee dem. So poor folks, dey ain' got-ee no coffee an' nothin'. We [make] de rice and make de coffee. Den we ain' got-ee no sugar, so we put de molasses in de coffee. Dat doan taste-ee so good, you understand me, but nobody can't do nothin' 'bout it.

"Captain Jim Meaher send word he doan want us to starve, you understand me, so he tell us to kill hogs. He say de hogs dey his and we his, and he doan want-ee no dead folks. Derefore you know we kill-ee hogs when we can't get-ee nothin'.

"When we at de plantation on Sunday we so glad we ain' got-ee no work to do. So we dance like in de Africa soil. De American colored folks, you understand me, dey say we savage and den dey laugh at us and doan come say nothin' to us. But Free George, you understand me, he a colored man doan belong to nobody. His wife, you understand me, she been free long time. So she cook for a Creole man and buy George because she marry wid him. Free George, he come to us and tell us not to dance on Sunday. Den he tell us whut Sunday is. We doan know whut it is before. Nobody in African soil doan tell us about no Sunday. Den we doan dance no mo' on de Sunday.

"Know how we get-ee free? Cudjo tell-ee you dat. De boat I was on, it in de Mobile. We all on dere to go in de Montgomery, but Captain Jim Meaher, he not on de boat dat day. Cudjo doan know (why). I doan forget. It April 12, 1865. De [Union] soldiers, dey come down to de boat and eat-ee de mulberries off de trees close to de boat, you understand me. Den dey see us on de boat and dey say 'Y'all can't stay dere no mo'. You free, you doan belong to nobody no mo'.'

"Oh, Lor'! I so glad. We ask de soldiers where we goin'? Dey say dey doan know. Dey told us to go where we feel like goin', we ain' [enslaved] no mo'.

"Thank de Lor'! I appreciate dey free me. Some de men dey on de steamboat in de Montgomery and dey got to come in de Mobile and unload de cargo. Den dey free too.

"We ain' got no trunk so we make de bundles. We ain' got no house so somebody tell-ee us come sleep-ee in de section house, a small building where railroad workers lived. We done dat till we could get-ee ourselves some place to go. Cudjo doan care—he a free man den."

"Now dey make us free but we ain' got no country and we ain' got no land!"

—*CUDJO LEWIS*

Chapter Eight

FREEDOM

"**AFTER DEY FREE US,** you understand me, we so glad. We make de drum and beat it like in de African soil. My countrymen come from Captain Burns Meaher plantation so we be together.

"We glad we free, but den, you understand me. We can't stay wid de folks [who don't] own us no mo'. Derefore, where we goin' live? We doan know. Some de folks from cross de water dey done marry and got de wife and children, you understand me.

Cudjo not marry yet. In de African soil when de man got-ee de wife, he build de house so dey live together and derefore de children come. So we want build-ee de houses for ourselves, but we ain' got no land. Where we goin' build-ee our houses?

"We meet together and we talk. We say we from cross de water so we go back where we come from. So we say we work in slavery five year and de six months for nothin'. Now we work for money and get-ee in de ship and go back to our country. We think Captain Meaher and Captain Foster ought take us back home. But we think we save money and buy de ticket ourselves. So we tell de women, 'Now we all want go back home. Somebody tell us it take lot of money to carry us back in de African soil. Derefore we got to work hard and save de money. You must help too. You see fine clothes, you must

122

not wish for dem.' De women tell us dey do all dey can to get back in dey country, and dey tell-ee us, 'You see fine clothes, don't you wish for dem neither.'

"We work hard and try save our money. But it too much money we need. So we think we stay here.

"We see we ain' got no ruler. Nobody to be de father to de rest. We ain' got no king neither no chief like in de Africa. We doan try get no king 'cause nobody among us ain' born no king. Dey tell us nobody doan have no king in American soil. Derefore we make Gumpa de head. He a nobleman back in Dahomey. We ain' mad wid him 'cause de king of Dahomey destroy our king and sell us to de White man. He didn't do nothin' against us.

"Derefore we join ourselves together to live. But we say, 'We ain' in de Africa soil no mo'. We ain' got-ee no land. Derefore we talk together so we say, 'Dey bring us away from our soil and work-ee us hard de five year and six months. We go to Captain Tim and Captain Jim and dey give us de land, so we make houses for ourself.'

"Dey say, 'Cudjo, you always talk-ee good, so you go tell de White men and tell-ee dem whut de African say.'

"All de Africans we work-ee hard, we get-ee work in de sawmill and de powder mill. Some us work for de railroad. De women work too so dey kin help us. Dey doing work for de White folks. Dey raise de garden and put de basket on de head and go in de Mobile and sell de vegetable. We make-ee de basket and de women sell-ee dem too.

"One day not long after, dey tell me to speak-ee for land so we build-ee our houses, Cudjo cuttin'

timber for de mill. It a place where de schoolhouse at now. Captain Tim Meaher come sit on de tree Cudjo just chop-ee down. I say, now is de time for Cudjo to speak-ee for his people. We want land so much I almost cry and derefore I stop-ee work and look-ee and look-ee at Captain Tim. He set on de tree choppin' splinters wid his pocket knife. When he don't hear de ax on de tree no mo', he look up and see Cudjo standin' dere. Derefore he ask me, 'Cudjo, what make you so sad?'

"I tell him, 'Captain Tim, I grieve for my home.' He say, 'But you got a good home, Cudjo.' Cudjo say, 'Captain Tim, how big is de Mobile?'

"'I doan know, Cudjo, I've never been to de four corners.'

"'Well, if you give Cudjo all de Mobile, dat railroad, and all de banks, Cudjo don't want it 'cause it ain' home. Captain Tim, you brought us from our country where we had land. You [enslaved] us. Now dey make us free but we ain' got no country and we ain' got no land! Why doan you give us piece dis land so we kin build-ee ourself a home?'

"Captain jump on his feet and say, 'Fool, do you think I goin' give you property on top of property? I don't owe [you] nothin.'"

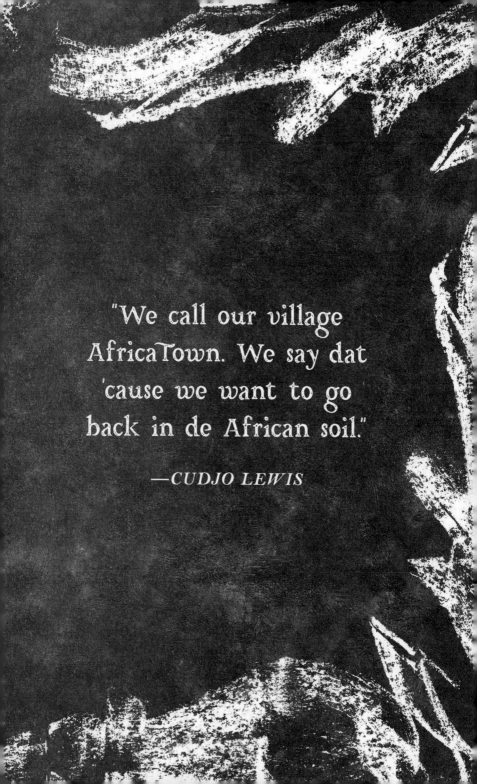

"We call our village AfricaTown. We say dat 'cause we want to go back in de African soil."

—CUDJO LEWIS

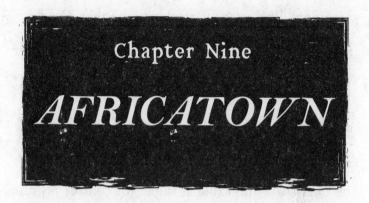

Chapter Nine

AFRICATOWN

"**CUDJO TELL GUMPA** (African Peter) call de people together, and he tell dem whut Captain Tim say. Dey say, 'Well we buy ourself a piece of land.'

"We work-ee hard and save, and eat molasses and bread and buy de land from de Meaher.

"We make Gumpa de head and Jaybee and Keebie de judges. Den we make laws how to behave ourselves. When anybody do wrong we make him appear befo' de judges and dey tell-ee him he got to stop doin' like dat 'cause it don't look nice. We don't want nobody to steal, neither get-ee drunk neither hurt-ee nobody. When we see a man drunk we say, 'Dere go de [enslaved person] whut beat his master.' Dat mean he buy de whiskey. It belong to him and he ought to rule it, but it done got control of him. Now thass right, ain' it?

"We build-ee de houses on de land we buy after we divide it up. Cudjo take one acre and de half for his part. We don't pay nobody build our houses. We all go together and build-ee de house for one another. So den we get-ee houses. Cudjo don't build-ee no house at first 'cause he ain' got no wife.

"We call our village AfricaTown. We say dat 'cause we want to go back in de African soil and we see we can't go. Derefore we make-ee de Africa

where dey fetch us. Gumpa say, 'My folks sell me and yo folks (Americans) buy me.' We here and we got to stay.

"Free George come help us all de time. De colored folks born here, dey pick at us all de time and call us ignorant savage. But Free George de best friend de Africans got. He tell us we ought get-ee de religion and join de church. But we don't want be mixed wid de other folks [who] laugh at us. So we say we got plenty land and derefore we kin build our own church. Derefore we go together and build-ee de Old Landmark Baptis' Church. It de first one round here."

Cudjo dismissed me by saying abruptly, "When you come tomorrow, I like you take me down de bay so we get-ee some crab."

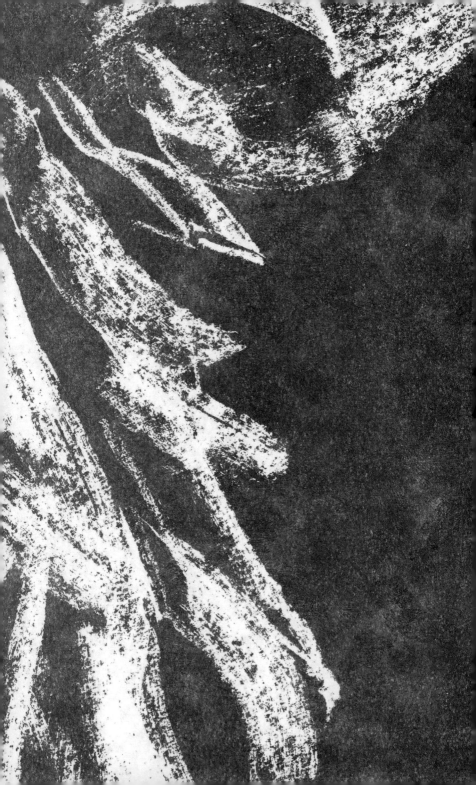

"... we do all we kin
to make happiness
between ourselves."

—CUDJO LEWIS

Chapter Ten

MARRIAGE

CUDJO HAD ON his battered hat when I drove up the next day. His rude walking stick was leaning against the door jamb. He picked it up and came on out to the car at once and we drove off. Without the least prompting he began to talk about his marriage.

"Abila, she a woman, you understand me, from cross de water. Dey call her Seely in American soil. I want dis woman to be my wife. She ain' married, you understand me, and I ain' get-ee no wife yet. All de folks from my country dey got family.

"Whut did Cudjo say so dat dis woman know he want to marry her? I tell-ee you dat. I tell-ee you de truth how it was.

"One day Cudjo say to her, 'I like-ee you to be my wife. I ain' got nobody.'

"She say, 'Whut you want wid me?'

"We got married one month after we agree between ourselves. We didn't had no wedding. Whether it was March or Christmas Day, I doan remember now.

"Derefore, you know, we live together, and we do all we kin to make happiness between ourselves.

"Derefore, you understand me, after me and my wife agree between ourselves, we seek-ee religion and got converted.

"Me and my wife, we have de six children together. Five boys and one girl. Oh, Lor'! Oh, Lor'! We so happy. Poor Cudjo! All de folks done left him now! I so lonely.

"We been married ten months when we have our first baby. We call him Yah-jimmy, just de same like we was in de African soil. For America we call him Aleck.

"In de Africa we got-ee one name, but in dis place dey tell us we need-ee two names. One for de son, you understand me, and den one for de father. Derefore I put de name of my father O-lo-loo-ay to my name. But it too long for de people to call it. It too [hard to say] like Kossula. So dey call me Cudjo Lewis.

"So you understand me, we give our children two names. One name because we not forget our home;

den another name for de American soil so it won't be too [hard] to call.

"De next child we name him Ah-no-no-toe. Den we call him Jimmy. De next one name Poe-lee-Dah-oo. He a boy, too. Den we have Ah-tenny-Ah and we call him David. De las' boy we call-ee him my name, Cudjo, but his African name, it Fish-ee-ton. Den my wife have one lil girl and we call her Ee-bew-o-see. Den we call her Seely after her mama.

"All de time de children growin,' de American folks dey picks at dem and tell de African people dey kill folks and eat-ee de meat. Dey call-ee my children ignorant savage and make out [as if] dey akin to monkey.

"Derefore, you understand me, my boys, dey fight. Dey got to fight all de time. Me and dey mama don't like to hear our children call savage. It hurt-ee dey feelings. Derefore dey fight. Dey fight hard. When dey whip de other boys, dey folks come to our house and tell-ee us, 'Yo' boys mighty bad, Cudjo. We afraid they goin' kill somebody.'

"Cudjo meet-ee de people at de gate and tell-ee dem, 'You see de rattlesnake in de woods?'

"Dey say, 'Yeah.'

"I say, 'If you bother wid him, he bite you. If you know de snake kill-ee you, why you bother wid him? Same way wid my boys, you understand me. If you leave my boys alone, dey not bother nobody!'

"Oh, Lor'! I love my children so much! I try so hard be good to our children. My baby, Seely, de only girl I got, she took-ee sick in de bed. Oh, Lor'! I do anything to save her. We get-ee de doctor. We get-ee all de medicine he tell-ee us to get. Oh, Lor'.

I pray, I tell de Lor' I do anything to save my baby life. She ain' but fifteen year old. But she die. Oh, Lor'! Look on de gravestone and see what it say. August de fifth, 1893. She born 1878. She don't have no time to live befo' she die. Her mama take it so hard. I try tell-ee her not to cry, but I cry too.

"Dat de first time in de American soil dat death find where my door is. But we from cross de water, know dat he come in de ship wid us. Derefore when we build-ee our church, we buy de ground to bury ourselves. It on de hill facin' de church door.

"We Christian people now, so we put our baby in de coffin and dey take her in de church, and everybody come look down in her face. Dey sing, 'Shall We Meet Beyond de River.' I been a member of de church a long time now, and I know de words of de song wid my mouth, but my heart it doan know dat.

Derefore I sing inside me, 'O todo ah wah n-law yah-lee, owrran k-nee ra ra k-nee ro ro.'

"We bury her dere in de family lot. She look-ee so lonesome out dere by herself—she such a lil girl, you understand me, dat I hurry and build de fence 'round de grave so she have protection.

"Nine year we hurt-ee inside 'bout our baby. Den we git hurt-ee again. Somebody call his-self a deputy sheriff kill de baby boy now.

"He say he de law, but he don't come arrest him. If my boy done something wrong, it his place come arrest him like a man. If he mad wid my Cudjo about something den he ought to come fight him face-to-face like a man. He don't come arrest him like no sheriff, and he doan come fight him like no man. He have words wid my boy, but he scared face him. Derefore, you understand me, he hide his-self in de butcher wagon and when it get-ee to my boy's store, Cudjo walk straight to talk business. Dis man, he hidin' his-self in de back of de wagon, an' shoot-ee my boy. Oh, Lor'! He shoot-ee my boy in de throat. He got no right shoot-ee my boy. He make out he scared my boy goin' shoot him and shoot-ee my boy down in de store. Oh, Lor'!

De people run come tell-ee me my boy hurt-ee. We took-ee him home and lay him in de bed. De big hole in de neck. He try so hard to catch-ee breath. Oh, Lor'! It hurt-ee me see my baby boy like dat. It hurt-ee his mama so her breast swell up so. It make me cry 'cause it hurt Seely so much. She keep standin' at de foot of de bed, you understand me, an' look-ee all de time in his face. She keep telling him all de time, 'Cudjo, Cudjo, Cudjo, baby, put whip to yo' horse!'

"He hurt-ee so hard, but he answer her de best he kin, you understand me. He tell-ee her, 'Mama, thass whut I been doin'!'

"Two days and two nights my boy lay in de bed wid de noise in de throat. His mama never leave him. She look-ee at his face and tell-ee him, 'Put whip to yo' horse, baby.'

"He pray all he could. His mama pray. I pray so hard, but he die. I so sad I wish I could die in place of my Cudjo. Maybe, I don't pray right, you understand me, 'cause he die while I was prayin' dat de Lor' spare my boy life.

"De man dat kill-ee my boy, he de pastor of Hay Chapel in Plateau today. I try forgive him. But Cudjo think that now he got religion, he ought to come and let me know his heart done change and beg Cudjo pardon for killin' my son.

"It only nine year since my girl die. Look like I still hear de bell toll for her, when it toll again for my Fish-ee-ton. My po' African boy dat don't never see African soil."

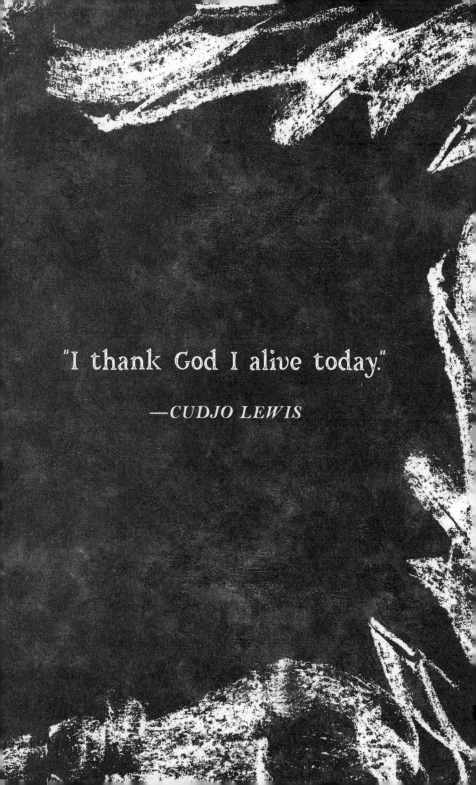

"I thank God I alive today."

—*CUDJO LEWIS*

Chapter Eleven

HURT

"DEY DOAN DO NOTHIN' to de man whut kill-ee my son.

"He a deputy sheriff. I doan do nothin'. I a Christian man den. I a sick man, too.

"Cudjo tell you how he git hurt-ee. I tell-ee you just like it were. Cudjo don't forget it.

"It in March, you understand me, and I make de garden. It de twelfth day of March 1902. A woman call me, you understand me, to plow de field for her.

She say, 'Cudjo, I like to git you plow de garden so I kin plant de sweet potatoes. I pay you.' I agree to dat.

"Derefore, you understand me, I get-ee up early de next mornin' and go plow de garden for her. So den when I git through wid hers, I kin plant my garden. I don't finish her garden 'cause my wife she call-ee me and scold me. She tell me, 'Cudjo, why you go work-ee hard like dat befo' you eat-ee your breakfast? Dat ain' right. You goin' be sick. I got-ee your breakfast ready long time. You come eat.'

"I go home wid Seely and eat-ee de breakfast. Den I think it goin' rain so I decide I plant my beans. Derefore, you understand me, I [ask] my wife come to de field wid me and help-ee me plant de beans.'

"She say, 'Cudjo, why you want me in de field? I can't plant no beans.'

"I tell her come on and drop de beans while I hill dem up. She come wid me and I show her how. After while she say, 'Cudjo, you don't need me drop no beans. You bring-ee me here for company.'

"I say, 'Thass right.'

"We ain' got enough beans. So I went to de market and ask de man for early beans, but he ain' got none. Derefore, you understand me, I get-ee my wife some meat and come home. Den I feed-ee my horse, an' my wife she cookin'. So den I brushed de horse and it sprinkle rain. I stop-ee and study. I don't know if I go get-ee mo' beans in de Mobile or if I wait. I decide to go fetch de beans. Derefore I ask my wife to give me money.

"She put three dollars on de mantelpiece. I ask her, 'Seely, why you give me so much-ee money? I don't need no three dollars.'

"She say, 'Spend whut you need and bring-ee de rest back. I know you ain' goin' waste de money.'

"Den I hitch up de horse and go in de Mobile to get-ee de beans. Soon as I get de beans I turn back to go home.

"When I reach-ee de Government Street and Common, it de L and N Railroad track dere, you understand me. When I approach de track, another [horse carriage] goin' very slow in de middle of de road. So I make de passee de [horse carriage] and just when I pass-ee it an' git out on de track, de train rush-ee down on me. Oh, Lor'! I holler to dem to stop 'cause I dere on de track, but dey don't stop. It a switch engine, you understand me. It rush-ee on and hit-ee de buggy an' knock me and hurt-ee my left side. Oh, Lor.' De horse get-ee scared and run away. My boy David find him next

day and fetch him home.

"Somebody see de train hit me and hear me hol-ler for dem to stop. Dey come pick-ee me up and carry me to de doctor office. He give me de [pain medicine]. A White lady on Government Street see me all hurt-ee and she see dat I [taken] care of. When I go home she send me a basket and visit me. She say de railroad ain' got no right smash up de buggy and hurt-ee me. I in de bed fourteen days. Dey broke three ribs. Dey ain' rung no bell. Dey ain' blow no whistle. She say she goin' see de com-pany. Derefore she go in de office of de L and N. De man in dere tell-ee her, 'We ain' goin' to do nothin'. It was daytime. Can't he see?'

"When I get able to get around de lady tell-ee me get me a lawyer and he make de company pay me for hurt-ee me and destroy de buggy.

"Derefore, I go in de office of Lawyer Clarke. He a big lawyer. Cudjo tell him, 'I ain' able to hire you. I want you to go to de company. I give you half.'

"De lawyer sue de company. De next year (1903) in January, dey send for me to appear in court. De judge say, 'De first case dis mornin' is Cudjo Lewis against de L an' N for five thousand dollars.'

"I look-ee hard. I say to myself, 'Who tell him dat? I didn't tell him I want five thousand dollars.'

"De railroad lawyer say, 'We ain' goin' to give him nothin'.'

"Well, Lawyer Clarke talk too. He say I all hurt-ee. I never be able to work no mo'. Dey pull off my short and look-ee at de left side and de doctor say, 'No, Cudjo can't work no mo'.' Den Lawyer Clarke say de railroad ought take care me—done [injure] me so bad.

"De railroad lawyer say dey not goin' give me nothin'. Dey say it broad daylight, ain' dis Cudjo got no eyes to see de great big train?

"Lawyer Clarke say, 'De train got a bell but dey didn't ring it. Dey got a whistle, but dey didn't blow it. De railroad track it layin' right cross de road. How kin de city of Mobile let-ee de company make de street dangerous and don't make dem pay when people git hurt-ee on dey track? He talk a long time. Den we all go out de courthouse to eat-ee de dinner.

"I tired, so I think I go home. I go get-ee some [meat] in de market to take home to Seely. David, he stay in de court. He know de market I like and derefore he run catch-ee me in de market 'fore I go home and tell me, 'Papa, de judge give you $650 from de company. De lawyer say you come tomorrow and get-ee yo' money.'

162

"I don't go next day, but I send David. De lawyer say dat too soon. Come back next week. Well, I send and I send, but Cudjo don't get-ee no money. In de 1904 de yellow fever come in de Mobile and Lawyer Clarke take his wife and children and get-ee on de train to run in de New York away from de fever, but he never get-ee in de North. He die on de way. Cudjo never know whut come of de money. It always a hidden mystery how come I not killed when de train it standing over me. I thank God I alive today.

"De people see I ain' able to work no mo', so dey make me de sexton of de church."

"One day we plant, de next we reap so we go on."

—CUDJO LEWIS

Chapter Twelve

LOSS

CUDJO'S FRIENDS DOWN the bay caught us a marvelous mess of blue crabs. We left these people late in the afternoon with many lingering exchanges of good wishes. On the way home we saw some excellent late watermelons in front of a store and bought two of them. I left one on his porch and took the other with me.

At the gate he called after me, "You come tomorrow and eat-ee de crab wid me. I like you come keep me comp'ny!"

So the next day about noon, I was sitting on his steps, between the rain barrels, eating crabs. When the crabs were gone, we talked.

"Let Cudjo tell-ee you about our boy, David. He such a good boy. Cudjo don't forget dat day. It Easter Saturday. He come home, you understand me, and find me sweepin' de church. I been de sexton long time den. So he ask me, 'Papa, where Mama?'

"I tell him, 'She in de house.'

"Derefore he go in de house, you understand me, and ask his mama what she goin' have for dinner. She tell-ee him she got de baked fish.

"He say, 'Oh, I so glad we got baked fish. Gimme my dinner quick.' His mama ask him, 'When did you ever see me give you anything to eat befo' your pa?' He say, 'Never.' She say, 'You take yo' bath den maybe dat time yo' pa here to eat-ee his dinner.'

"De boy run-ee back out to me and tell me make haste so he get something to eat. He hungry. I chop-ee de wood so he take de ax and chop-ee de wood his-self. I say, 'Go on, son, I ain' weak yet. I kin chop dis wood!' He say, 'No, I don't want you chop wood and I right here and strong.' Derefore he chop-pee de wood and carry it in de house where his ma can reach-ee it.

"Den we eat our dinner and David wash-ee his-self and his mama put out de clean clothes for him to put on. He got on de undershirt, but he ain' got on de top shirt. He ain' got no button on de under-shirt so me and his ma see de flesh. So I say, 'Son, fasten yo' clothes so yo' mama don't see de skin.'

"He look-ee at his-self den he ask me, 'Who first saw me naked? My ma.' Den he laugh and put on de rest of de clothes. He say, 'Papa, Mama, I go in de Mobile and get-ee de laundry. Den I have clean shirts.'

"I ask him, 'How long befo' you come from town?' He say, 'Not long. Maybe I catch-ee de same car back.'

"So he go leave de house.

"After while we hear somebody dey come laughing and talking. Seely say, 'David got a friend wid him.' I look-ee to see who David got wid him, but it ain' David.

"Two men come tell me, 'Uncle Cudjo, yo' boy dead in Plateau.'

"I say, 'My boy not in Plateau. He in de Mobile.' Dey say, 'No, de train kill yo' boy in Plateau.'

"I tell dem, 'How kin de train kill my David in Plateau when he not dere? He gone in de Mobile to get his laundry. He be back after while.'

"Seely say, 'Go see, Cudjo. Maybe it not our boy. Go see who get killed.'

"Den I ask de men, 'Where dat man get killed you tell-ee me about?'

"Dey say, 'On de railroad track in Plateau.'

"Derefore, you understand me, I go follow de people. Then I get-ee to de place wid de big crowd and stand around and look-ee.

"I go through de crowd and look-ee. I see de body of a man by de telegraph pole. Somebody tell me, 'Thass yo' boy, Uncle Cudjo.' I say, 'No, it not my David.' One woman she face me and ask, 'Cudjo, which son of yours is dis?' and she point-ee at de body. I tell her, 'Dis none of my son. My boy go in town and y'all tell me my boy dead.'

"Somebody ask me, 'Cudjo, yo' boy dead. Must I toll de bell for you? You de sexton. You toll de bell for everybody else, you want me toll it for David?'

"I ask him, 'Why you want to toll de bell for David? He ain' dead.'

"De African man told de people pick up de body and carry it home. So dey took de window shutter and lay de body on it and fetch it to Cudjo's gate. De gate, it too small, so dey lift it over de gate and place it on de porch. I so worried. I wish-ee so bad my David come back from town so de people stop sayin' dat my son on de shutter.

"When dey place de shutter on de porch, my wife she scream and fall out. De African man say again, 'Cudjo, thass yo' boy.' I look-ee down in David face. Den I say to de crowd, 'Git off my porch! Git out my yard!'

"Dey went. Den I fell down and open de shirt and push-ee my hand in de bosom and feel de marks.

And I know it my son. I tell dem toll de bell.

"My wife look-ee at my face and she scream and scream and fell on de floor and can't raise herself up. I run-ee out de place and fell on my face in de pine grove. Oh, Lor'! I stay dere. I hurt-ee so. It hurt-ee me so to hear Seely cry. Those who had come cross de water come to me. They say, 'Uncle Cudjo, come home. Yo' wife want you.' I say, 'Tell Seely doan holler no mo'. I can't stand it.'

"She promise me she won't holler if I come home. So I got back to de house.

"De bell toll again.

"Our house, it very sad. Look-ee like all de family hurry to leave and go sleep on de hill.

"Poe-lee very mad 'cause de railroad kill his brother. He want me to sue de company. I ask him, 'Whut for? We doan know de White folks' law.

Dey say dey don't pay you when dey hurt-ee you. De court say dey got to pay you de money. But dey ain' done it.' I very sad. Poe-lee very mad. He say de deputy kill his baby brother. Den de train kill David. He want to do something.

"But I ain' hold no malice. De Bible say not. Poe-lee say in African soil it ain' lak in de America. He ain' been in de Africa, you understand me, but he hear what we tell-ee him and he think dat better dan where he at. Me and his mama try to talk to him and make him satisfy, but he don't want hear nothin'. He say when he a boy, dey [Americans] fight him and say he a savage. When he get-ee a man dey cheat him. De train hurt-ee his papa and don't pay him. His brothers get-ee kill. He don't laugh no mo'.

"Well, after while, you understand me, one day

he say he go catch-ee some fish. Somebody see him go towards de Twelve Mile Creek. Lor', Lor'! He never come back."

There was a muted mournful pause, in which I could do nothing but wait with my eyes in the China-berry tree lest I appear too nosy. Finally he came back to me.

"Excuse me I can't help it I cry. I lonesome for my boy. Cudjo know dey doan do in de American soil like dey do cross de water, but I can't help dat. My boy gone. He ain' in de house and he ain' on de hill wid his mama. We both miss-ee him. I don't know. Maybe dey kill my boy. It a hidden mystery. So many de folks dey hate my boy 'cause he like his brothers. Dey don't let nobody abuse dem like dey dogs. Maybe he in de African soil like somebody say. Po' Cudjo lonesome for him, but Cudjo don't know.

"I try be very nice to Seely. She de mama, you understand me, and derefore, you know she grieve so hard about her children. I always try please her, you understand me. But when we ain' got but two our children wid us, I can't stand see her look so like she want cry all de time. We ain' got but one child in de house wid us, 'cause Aleck, dat de oldest one, you understand me, he married and live wid his wife. We build-ee him a house right in de yard, just like in de African soil.

"Look like we ain' cry enough. We ain' through cryin'. In de November our Jimmy come home and set round like he doan feel good so I ask him, 'Son, you get-ee sick? I don't want you runnin' to work when you doan feel good.' He say, 'Papa, ain' nothin' wrong wid me. I don't feel so good.' But de next day, he come home sick and we put-ee him in de bed. I do all I kin and his mama stay up wid him all night long. We get-ee de doctor and do whut he say, but our boy die.

"Oh Lor'! I good to my children! I want dey company, but look-ee like dey lonesome for one another. So dey hurry go sleep together in de graveyard. He die holdin' my hand.

"When we get-ee back from de funeral, ain' nobody in de house but me and Seely. De house was full, but now it empty. We old folks now and we know we ain' going have no mo' children. We so lonesome, but we know we can't get-ee back de dead. When de spit goes from de mouth, it doan come back. When de earth eats, it don't give back. So we try to keep one another company and be happy.

"I still sexton of de church. It growing to be a

big church now. We call it de Old Landmark Baptis' Church, 'cause it de first one in AfricaTown. Dey done build mo' Baptis' churches now, but ours, it de first.

"My wife she help me all she kin. She don't let me strain myself so I hurt-ee de side where de train hit-ee me.

"One day we plant, de next we reap so we go on."

Before I left, I had Kossula's permission to photograph him. But he forbade my coming back within three days. A cow had broken in his fence and was eating his potato vines.

It was on a hot Saturday afternoon that I came to photograph Kossula.

"I'm glad you take my picture. I want see how I look. Once long time ago somebody come take my

picture but they never give me one. You give me one."

I agreed. He went inside to dress for the picture. When he came out, I saw that he had put on his best suit but removed his shoes. "I want to look like I in Africa, 'cause dat where I want to be," he explained.

He also asked to be photographed in the cemetery among the graves of his family.

"I got nobody. . . ."

—*CUDJO LEWIS*

Chapter Thirteen

ALONE

"**ONE NIGHT SEELY WAKE** up in de night and say, 'Cudjo, wake up. I dream about our children. Look like dey cold.' I tell her she think too much. Go back to sleep.

"It hurt-ee me, 'cause it a cold night in November in de 1908 and I remember how Seely used to visit de children when dey was little to see dey got plenty quilts, so dey keep warm, you understand me. De next day, she say 'Cudjo, come on go see our children's grave. So I say yes, but I try not take her 'cause I afraid she worry about dem.

"So I go in de church and make like I busy so she forget de graveyard. When I come out de church, I don't see her nowhere, so I look cross de hill and I see her in de family lot. I see Seely goin' from one her children grave to de other, like she cover dem up wid mo' quilts.

"De next week my wife left me. Cudjo don't know. She ain' been sick, but she die. She don't want to leave me. She cry 'cause she don't want me be lonesome. But she leave me and go where her children [are]. Oh, Lor'! Lor'! De wife de eyes to de man's soul. How kin I see now, when I ain' got-ee de eyes no mo'?

"De next month my Aleck he die. Den I just like I come from de African soil. I got nobody but de daughter-in-law, Mary, and de grandchildren. I tell-ee her she my son's wife so she stay in de compound and she take de land when I go wid Seely and our children.

"I appreciate my countrymen; dey come see me when dey know I lonely. Another time dey come to me and say, 'Uncle Cudjo, make us another parable.'

"I bow my head in my hands, den I lift it up again." It was his characteristic gesture when he begins a story.

"Den I talk. 'I don't know—me and my wife, we been ridin'. I think we go to Mount Vernon. De conductor go to her and say, 'Ole Lady, where you goin' get off?' She say, 'Plateau.'

"I look at her. I say, 'How you say you goin' get off at Plateau? I thought you goin' to Mount Vernon wid me.'

"She shake her head. She say, 'I don't know. I just know I get off at Plateau. I don't wanna leave you, but I got to get off at Plateau.'

"De conductor blow once. He blow twice, and my wife she say, 'Goodbye, Cudjo. I hate to leave you.' But she git off at Plateau. De conductor come to me and ask, 'Ole man, where you goin' git off?'

"I say, 'Mount Vernon.'

"I traveling yet. When I get to Mount Vernon, I no talk to you no mo'.'"

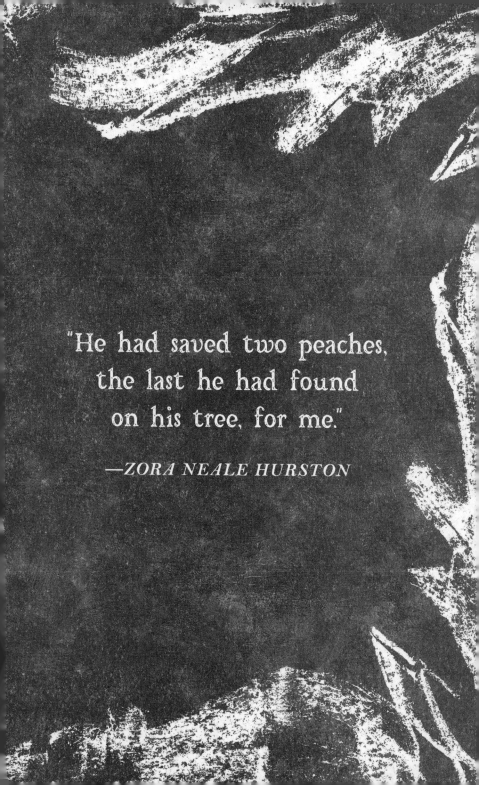

"He had saved two peaches,
the last he had found
on his tree, for me."

—ZORA NEALE HURSTON

Chapter Fourteen

GOODBYE

I HAD SPENT two months with Kossula, who is called Cudjo, trying to find the answers to my questions. Some days we ate great quantities of peaches and talked. Sometimes we ate watermelon and talked. Once it was a huge mess of steamed crabs. Sometimes we just ate. Sometimes we just talked. At other times neither was possible, he just chased me away. He wanted to work in his garden or fix his fences. He couldn't be bothered. The present was too urgent to let the past intrude. But on the whole, he was glad to see me, and we became warm friends.

At the end, the bond had become strong enough for him to wish to follow me to New York. It was a very sad morning in October when I said the final goodbye and looked back the last time at the lonely figure that stood on the edge of the cliff that fronts the highway. He had come out to the front of his place that overhangs the Cochrane Highway that leads to the bridge of that name. He wanted to see the last of me. He had saved two peaches, the last he had found on his tree, for me.

When I crossed the bridge, I know he went back to his porch; to his house full of thoughts. To his memories of girls in West Africa with ringing golden bracelets, his drums that speak the minds of men, to palm-nut cakes, to his smoke pictures, to his parables.

I am sure that he does not fear death. But he is full of trembling awe before the altar of the past.